Sweet WINTER

A FEW WORDS FIRST

In my family — especially my mom, they're in love with Christmas and holidays. My favorite holidays are Halloween and Thanksgiving. So, I kinda wanted to bring something to life that was in the middle. I really hope you will enjoy this book, I know it was fun for me to write!

Thank you for following for all of those years and to you who just begun. Here's to another one!

To my best friend Laura, I keep on saying that those books would not be without you and it became even more true. Thank you for your support and immense help, through thick and thin, we are in this together.

Love, always,

Chrys.

OTHER WORK

Poems & Short Stories Series:

POEMS: PART I

SHORT STORIES: PART I

POEMS: PART II

Upcoming:

SHORT STORIES: PART II

You can find more info at chrystelemyriamuni.com

To contact Chrystele Myriam: contactinfo@chrystelemyriamuni.com

Index

CHILL

Snow around me

Winter whispering to my heart

Sweet and chill

In the middle of nowhere

On my warm bed I lay there still

CLOSED DOOR

Of all of the people I wished to see

Wished to hold

Wished to cherish

Your face was not the one I was ready for

The time spent apart was a shot to my heart

So don't hate me for doing this

For I this time will be the one to close the door

Prison Cell

"Well, this is a nice change of scenery.", "This is a prison cell.", "I was being sarcastic.", "You know—I just— I don't get you! It's New Year's Eve and we are stuck here because of you, yet you still find a way to make me angrier!", "Hey! I just wanted to dance, okay?", "Did you really have to kick this cop out of the way?", "Yeah! I could've made the cut for the new year's special!", "Well, now you've got your face up there. Stupid Christmas, and crappy new year. That's how this year ends and new year begins. I hate you.", "No you don't."

APOCALYPTIC WASTELAND

Everything was perfect. From the moment that I won this price to the time I got into the plane on my way back home. What we all witnessed once we arrived was chilling and it was not because of the weather. No one was here to greet us, to help us get our package. Everyone in the plane, including the airline employees were shocked and unaware of what was before our eyes. It was the kind of desert that you knew, that you could feel deep down in your guts that there was something behind it. Either there has been a storm, an upcoming one, or it's still ongoing. Unfortunately for me, I had a sick feeling this storm was still there, and little did I know, I was in the eye of it. Little did I know, it was Armageddon.

I was so happy for this Christmas. It was the first one I was spending alone, and I decided to take a chance and do this giveaway for a free trip. I never thought I would win and when I did, I actually checked multiple times to see if it was a scam or not. It was the last happy and calm I got ever since. I have been fighting each day for my life, for food, for shelter. Anything that could help me survive and live another day.

This cold winter was the perfect weather if you'd think about spending holidays, but the only remaining and traces of what could have been was broken decorations and burnt trees. People were going through the houses that were abandoned or the owners were dead and stole everything they could carry.

There could have been something like in the movies, clans born from this apocalyptic world, but no. It was each to their own.

I was alone before, I knew how to fight for myself, but this time it was different. This time I was too much alone, and it was scary, impossible to sleep and hard to breathe.

ROYALTY

(Explicit)

Baby you know I'm royalty,

If you're lucky I'll let you under me,

Something about me is healing,

My time is free,

No need to think about it,

Don't fuck this up, but you can fuck me

Taste you from morning till dawn in front of the chimney

Christmas present

Giving you this body

Waves and crashing through this feeling

I came to impress

Pack a suitcase and let's get locked up together

We ain't like others

Leaving the sheets for later

Let's do it our way, making memories in this house

Showing you all of my dirty truth while I'm under you

No visits. Nothing. Not even a trace of him being there. I'm not one to get revenge, but I'm petty. And this level of petty I've reached was legendary. As I packed my bags and sang Christmas carols, I had a smile on my lips.

Landing finally, I hurried off to my destination, one goal in mind. I knocked on the door, luggage still next to me. "Hi! What can I do for you?", "I'd like to see Mr. Claus, please.", "Oh, I'm sorry but he is resting.", "I'm sure he is, but this very important.", "Okay, let me see what I can do."

After a while she finally let me in his office. "What can I do for you?", "Well, you forgot to visit my house this Christmas." He frowned, "that is impossible.", "My kid cried and cried and cried because Santa — you — forgot us. So, I came here for an explanation as to why you did not come.", "I never forget houses.", "Nick, let me get this straight, I will not come back home until you made this better. Check for yourself and see." He did so and looked even more confused. "I—I do not see your house." I frowned, "what?" He showed me his map, and indeed our house or our existence was unknown from his magic. "How is that possible?", "The last time it happened it was because... no. It's not possible.", "What?", "Your son is going to be my replacement."

ABOMINABLE SNOWMAN

"Mom! Mom! Tell me the story again!", "Okay, one more time, but then we go to sleep!", "Yes! Please!"

It was approaching Christmas. All was white and cold. The chill winter made everything perfect for little kids to play outside and build snowmen while the parents stayed inside preparing the festivities.

But one day, one special little kid named Alex made a very beautiful snowman. Sadly for Alex, everyone found the snowman scary. He was not loved from the others, not even Alex's parents. So an evening, tears rolling down Alex's cheeks, the child kicked the snowman and destroyed it while saying how much they hated it.

Christmas is a period charged with magic, and things that usually don't happen; happen during this time. And so during the night, the snowman came back to life half destroyed. Angry, the snowman swore to seek revenge on everyone that hated him and made its creator cry and despise him.

When Alex woke up the snowman was gone, making nothing of it either than just the snow melting, everyone went on with their lives. Much to their demises, the news of kids disappearing came through. Each hour new children were missing. Christmas was close, it was three days away and little did everyone know, Christmas Day had an important role to play in this.

"How important mommy?", "Well, Alex had to find the abominable snowman before Christmas and stop him."

Because this child was the only one to be able to stop the snowman, if the snowman was not to be stopped before Christmas, it would be impossible to destroy him. 'I need to find him,' thought Alex. So on in this adventure, with just a backpack, Alex went on to search for the snowman. After a moment, and nothing new, Alex started to lose hope.

Snow arrived, Alex looked up and said, "Dear Santa, please help me find the mean snowman so I can save my friends and spend a happy Christmas with my family." Alex found shelter and waited for the snow to stop. After a while Alex departed again and found his way to a house that was open, when entering the house Alex found two other little kids, or that was what Alex thought at first. "Hello!" Said one the kids. "My name is Andrew and next to me is Alicia!", "Hi?" Alex was a bit weirded out by how joyful the kids were. "We heard you needed help." Said the little girl. "That's right, Santa sent us." Alex was shocked, "He sent you?", "Of course. Santa heard your prayer. We knew how noble your cause is.", "Yes indeed, so here we are.", "You're elves?" The kids laughed, "Not really. We are kids, well, we live as children for eternity, but no, we are not elves. Those are just tales.", "So you're old?", "Very. Small but mighty!" The little girl got closer to Alex, "And so are you. We will help you find the snowman before Christmas. Let's go, we know where he might be."

"Mom! Do you think I could become Santa's helper and stay forever a kid?", "If you are good enough each year, maybe!", "What happened next, mom?", "Well, off to the destination where the snowman was hiding the three children gathered their courage and faced him!", "Did they win?", "Of course they did, baby. And they were able to bring back all the children to their homes.", "How did they defeat the snowman?",

Sweet Winter

At the piano sat an old lady, playing 'The First Noel' with tears rolling down her eyes, and memories flooding her mind, she patiently waited for her daughter and her family to arrive. She looked up at the picture frame on the piano and smiles, "Oh Robert. Fortieth Christmas without you. I miss you, dear." She finished the song when she heard the door open and kids running in, "Grandma! Grandma!", "Granny! We've got so many gifts for you from Santa!" She smiled, "Do you now? And are any of them hugs and kisses?" They laughed and went to greet her. Her daughter and son-in-law entered, "Hey, mom. There was this card in the mailbox." She handed it to her mother, and her heart stopped. "It's your father's handwriting.", "What?"

"Dear Melanie, my one true love. I know I am going to be home for Christmas, in two days, but I still wanted to send you this card. It made me think of you, bright and beautiful. I can't wait to see you.

I love you.

Always yours, Rob."

"It... it was the Christmas that he never got home. The card he sent before..." With shaking hands she looked at her daughter and son-in-law that were both crying. "Mom, are you okay?", "Yes. That was my sign. I asked for a sign that he was still there. And somehow, your father still finds a way to make winter a sweet season.", "It was forty years ago, though. It's..." The son-in-law did not finish the sentence, "Well, Melanie, Merry Christmas from Robert.", "He made it home for Christmas." Her daughter held her, "Yes he did mom. He made it home."

DIFFERENT

Expectations and hope

Sometimes life comes knocking at the door

Out of the blue and often cruel

To all of you who spends a Christmas not planned

Hold each other's hand

You're together and that is what matters

If this year taught us something

Is unity and family

Look at the sky up above and be grateful for love

Tough times are in the past and ahead of you

Believe you will come through

And if you have doubt

I will fight with you

"We will be snowed in up here for several days at least," said Carrie. "What in the world are we going to do to entertain ourselves?", "Well, we still have to figure out who dropped the body in front of the city hall's Christmas tree.", "How do you want to investigate if we're all secluded?", "We can try.", "Fine. What do we know so far?", "The victim is a white male. Around mid-thirties. It was not a robbery gone bad. No valuable objects missing.", "Yeah, the way the corps was placed next to the tree it almost feels… meaningful.", "We can try and see if there has been any similar cases.", "Yeah do that while I search a little bit more on our victim so I can make up a profile."

After hours of working, they came up with ten similar cases and ten similar profiles. "So, all male, white, mid-thirties, placed in the same position next to a city hall's Christmas tree.", "Yes, but we're stuck and there is nothing we can do. At least nothing more than that. The murderer is here in town as the last victim was right before the snow storm, so he or she is stuck just as us. Once we're out, we have to move fast before they do."

The next day the storm stopped and they were able to get out. They went to the precinct as fast as they could and searched through the security cameras scattered around the city to pin point the murderer. "Okay, so the victim was seen here before being killed. That is the last appearance.", "Can you try and go backward on his day and see if there is someone appearing all the time or almost?", "Sure.", "We need to find someone, a recurring face will be enough for us. We need a lead. If you do find someone, try and see if you see that person near the other victims." The man sitting on the chair started the facial recognition software. "How does this work?", "Well, it measures the structure of each face, including distance between eyes, nose, mouth and jaw to create a facial template. Where it finds a match, it sends an alert to officers on the scene. This will take more time, though, I'm running it for multiple cities.", "We don't have much time. We cannot let him or her drop another body. Christmas is approaching, we cannot let that happen." Someone entered the room, frantic. "It's too late. A body was found in front of a Christmas tree of a shopping mall.", "Here in Manhattan?", "Yes. Fulton Center.", "Run the facial recognition now around the perimeter. We will go on the scene and get you the footage quickly." The man on the chair nodded. Carrie and her partner left the precinct and went to the Fulton Center. When they arrived, the place was surrounded by police and people that were watching, filming what was happening. They met with the medical examiner that was already on the scene. "What do we have?", "White male, mid-thirties. Same position as the others, nothing stolen.", "How long has he been dead?", "Judging by the temperature of the body and how cold it was last night, probably five hours ago.", "The mall was closed. So the murderer found a way to get in. Okay. Any prints?", "Partial ones. But I'll have to check that at the lab.", "Thanks doc." They got in the shopping mall to talk to the manager. "Hi. Your colleagues told me that you'd need the footages," he handed them multiple cassettes. "Here. It's from the closure of last night to now.", "Thank you. I know our colleagues asked you questions but we need to, too." The manager nodded. "Have you seen anything suspicious yesterday?", "No. I was not there yesterday. But I can send you the names of who was there the whole day and who closed. I have the book where they sign each time they close the mall.", "Thank you."

"With the footage that you got from the mall and the ones of the previous murders, so far I found no one that comes back more than once. Not enough to make it suspicious.", "Okay. This person is smart. No prints so far, nothing on the cameras, no witnesses. Nothing.", "Have we tried looking at the missing persons that matches our victims' type?", "I'm on it." On a screen was seen a search scan through a system named COMPACT. After a few minutes eight missing persons' faces where on the big screen. "So we have eight potential victims. Can you find a pattern? We need to profile the murder. If we want to catch them we need to understand them. We are running out of time."

"Judging from what you told me," started the profiler, "this murder is very confident. Dropping corps in public places where he can get caught, where there are a lot of people passing by, he has a profound trust in his abilities. It can either mean he has a huge ego, or that he's trained. The fact that it's around Christmas and he's dropping them next to a Christmas tree, in a sort of a cross, it's significant. As if it was sacrifices.", "Religious crimes?", "Not necessarily. Can be vengeful. Something that happened in his life around holidays. I'd need to know more to be able to profile him, or her.", "On that matter, do you think it's a woman or a man?", "There is a lot to take in for that. We'd have to know more. But at this rate it could be both. Male are six times as likely to kill a stranger. But women are twice as likely to kill a person that they know or encountered. Men tend to stalk their victims, there is also a sexual tension in most of the murderers. Not necessarily rape, but something that brings to sexuality, a position, an object, some clothes being ripped. When it's a woman, there more of a 'reason,' behind it such as money, convenience, revenge. From what we know, it could be both. It could be someone that is the exception to the rule.", "Is there any indication of being multiple murderers?", "It does not seem like it. There is a pattern in the killing, in each city there are two murders, then he goes to another city.", "And he just killed the second victim here in Manhattan. We need to hurry. How long is the time laps before the new killings?", "Five days.", "Okay, search in the victims' lives and the missing persons lives' something that connects them. A place, a person. Maybe they go to the same church, maybe to the same market, part of a clan. Just something to create a string that will lead us to whoever is doing this."

"You were right. They all went to the same place. The same after school church class.", "Now we've got something. What else did you find?", "Well, apart from two people who worked there died, we have potentials murderers.", "Okay, run their faces on the facial recognition side to side with the footages and see if you find any match."

"We've got four suspects that could have done it based on their backgrounds. But there is one that matched the facial recognition 6 times out of ten.", "What about the missing persons? Any connection?", "Not that we know of, no."," Okay. Let's focus on our dead ones then.", "Six out of ten you said, who is it?", "It's a woman, mid-thirties too, white. Emily McLain. She went to school with them.", "What makes her our prime suspect?", "She filed a report against them for collective rape." All of the agents fell silent. "So we are looking for revenge. Where is she now?", "I'm having a hard time to find her in any security cameras. I found her address and relatives information. I sent it to you." Carrie and her partner nodded and went to their car on their way to Emily's house. "If what happened is true—", "If? After all of those years, she is still seeking revenge. She lived in the past for so many years. Impossible to move on from it. If did not happen, it's still happening to her, in her mind. She's reliving it all each day, and she probably thinks that if they're all dead maybe it'll make it better.", "Well, she will be the one to end up in jail.", "Yeah, because our system failed her."

Once they arrived to the place they knocked on the door, "Emily McLain, this the FBI, please open the door. Go check the back to see if she goes out." Her partner nodded. "Emily, if you're in there, please let me in, just me. I believe you. I know what happened to you, and I am so sorry. Our justice failed you. I know you think it will make it all better but it will not. Do not let them win, not again. Please." The door slowly creaked open, Carrie put her gun in the holster and went in, her partner standing by. "Hi. My name is Carrie." Emily was sitting on a chair, her gun to her head. "Please, put the gun down.", "Why? So you can lock me up instead of locking them?", "I know this is not fair, I know. But please, don't. You still have a life.", "Oh, really? I'm not dumb you know. I know I will go for life in prison, if not death penalty. I won't die there, not amongst them.", "You're right. You're not like them," she slowly walked, step by step, hands in the air towards Emily. "Do not come closer or I swear I will shoot myself." Carrie stopped. "Okay, okay.", "They deserved to die! After what they did to me... What would you have done?", "I... I can't put myself at your place. I can't.", "Exactly. So stop saying that you know or understand. You don't.", "You're right. But please, hear me out. We can still get justice for what happened to you. We can still try and this time I will help you.", "It's too late! Nobody will hear me, nobody did hear me. I'm done. You can't help me. I see that you want to, and thank you. But you can't I'm gone. I'm done." And just like that, Emily shot herself in the head.

PRACTICE MAKES PERFECT

She kept playing and playing the violin. Playing on repeat Adagio in E Major, K. 261 until she could no longer feel her fingers or felt blood trickle down, only then she would stop playing. She was getting ready for her Christmas concert, a professor from the Juilliard school was going to be there, it was her chance to get noticed. When she finished the last bit of the song, her blood chilled. Someone was clapping. She turned around and saw no one. How could that be? She was alone, or at least she thought. She put down her violin and took a look around the house to see if there were any windows open and she might just have heard a neighbor applaud her. But when she got back to her living room, the violin was playing the same song, on its own.

WILLING AND ABLE

Cain and Abel

Willing and able

Out for a victim

Out for a crime scene

Seek violence

Crave blood

As I roam the earth

A good and lost soul responds

Hello there sweet one

Let me rip your fingers one by one

What's that now?

Holidays makes you sick?

No worries I'm here

I'm your salvation

Murderers don't take vacations

WRITERS

Be careful as for us writers

Love to create

We create worlds and characters

But sometimes we use reality as inspiration

An individual might entertain us

Then we take the essence and put it into a story

Don't worry though

As from the moment we write about you

You will live forever

Through space and time

Your memory will be down on paper

Ink and souvenirs

BETRAYAL

From the very beginning I had guarded my heart, I had it on lock. But with her it was different. I did not have to hide who I was. I never thought she would be the one to betray me like that. I had no idea of who she was, but only who she was pretending to be. "Why?" I asked as tears rolled down my cheek, "Because last Christmas you fired my brother, and this Christmas, I got my revenge.", "Revenge? I fired him, you killed my brother!", "Yes, and now we are quit.", "No were not!", "Oh come on, you should thank me, you will no longer be the little sister in her big brother's shadow.", "No. But I will be the one to get my revenge. You're dead to me, but first, your family is at the top of the list." The other woman laughed. "Oh, how sweet. You will do none of that. Wanna know why?" A pause, "Because I made you fall in love with me."

NATIVITY

Have you heard about the legend? This crazy and chilling legend that touches only cursed families. Families all around the globe only at Christmas.

Each figurine in the nativity scene was replaced. One by one, right before the body was found, a figurine looking like the victim would appear. And just like that, the whole family was frozen forever in figurines, without everyone noticing. And it will go on like this, until the next family and the next, and so on.

And this year would be this new family's first Christmas at the house, and they would discover the nativity scene, and soon become part of it.

WINTERBOURNE

Floating away

Season of cold,

Season of white

Snow and slow

I'm just like this flow

I'm there for an amount of time

And then I sublime,

In the summer I hide,

Dry and tired

I rest and assess

Will I come back in following winter

Or will I go on away forever

Distressed and oppressed

Those changes are challenges

My flow varies

My tears this steam carries

WOLVES

For all of these years I was looking for them I never found a single trace, no lead. Nothing. I knew they were not dead; my heart knew it. And since they left, my heart kept dreaming of them, them coming back to me, over and over. Time is supposed to heal, but this hole burning in my heart was there. And the chill winter was not helping to extinguish it. Out in the cold winter and snowed ground, I went into the forest. Something we loved to do together. The whole time I felt like I was followed, being watched. And as I turned around for the fifth time, I saw two wolves. And then I knew. I knew them, their eyes, their soul. They were not afraid, neither was I. We knew each other. They were my brothers.

My heart broke. Everything we built and were supposed to build together went to smoke when I realized that I would never get them back. Sinking onto my knees I cried. "No. This not fair. You left me!" And all over again my heart broke, and the burn went on faster, deeper.

Silenced scream

What good is a banshee who has been rendered mute you ask? She has been tortured, put into a cell and then another. She was torn apart, killed, and brought back to life. It's a sin how much she survived. No sound coming out of her mouth, but wrath coming out of her soul.

And as she opened her mouth, the whole world shook, the snow melted and winter was changed into a dark burning abyss. They didn't quite succeed to mute her. Of all of the things they did to her, she had bigger plans. And no matter what or where she planned to do it, it would be a sin. She tried to not to do it, but blood spilled. Contrast of red on white.

They didn't believe it, but they created a monster. "Father oh father, forgive me for I have sinned. I do not understand yet, but I'm louder than I ever been before." And her prayer was heard by every celestial being.

BLOODSHED

Magic in the air, Christmas lights and hope. It was perfect. As she paced back and forth she knew, "it's time." She transformed into a black serpent and hissed. The plan was in action. There was one more thing needed. She needed a shocking act of bloodshed to inspire the uprising, and she knew where to get it and when.

The Church was celebrating Christmas, the children choir was performing, everyone was clapping and singing along, and then, silence.

Scream. Fear.

A black serpent appeared then changed into a woman who was smiling. "Now, now. Let me finish what I begun at the beginning of time. End this." All of the guests in the church began to cough on blood then fall to the ground one by one. When the last body dropped onto the floor, the ground shook. "That's it. Rise up my children." Dark shadows flew around her. "Go out, find them all, kill them all. Every last of them. Make my father regret banishing me from Eden. Make him cry, make him beg."

"There is one last thing left for the potion to work its way and the spell will be ready to finish your transition for the full moon on thanksgiving.", "What is it?", "Angel feather. Just one. I know where to find it, but the place where it is, is… Hard to reach. Only you have to get it, but only me can reach this place.", "Where is it?", "The black market. It's on the open ocean.", "Wait, what? Isn't there another market?", "In this realm? I'm afraid not. And we need a feather from this realm, or it will not work.", "Fine. Tell me what I need to do?", "Kill me, then drink my blood. Once you've done this, you will get my powers and be able to get it. Once you get the feather, follow the instructions I gave you, and you will transform on thanksgiving as soon as the full moon rises.", "Are you sure about that?", "Yes. But be careful when you get to the market, you will know you're close when the path changes course as you will walk on it. It's to try to make you change your mind, or get lost. Only someone like me can deceive it. As you will have my blood run through your veins, you will be able to access to the market.", "After the transition I won't need your blood to access to anything, I will own this realm and be undefeatable.", "Yes you will, my Lord."